BÊTE NOIRE

FEAR IS JUST A POINT OF VIEW

Editors:

A. W. Gifford

Jennifer L. Gifford

P.O. Box 811
Ortonville, MI 48462

www.betenoiremagazine.com

Bête Noire is published by Dark Opus Press a division of Charm Noir Omnimedia P.O Box 811, Ortonville, MI 48062

ISBN-13: 978-0692467121
ISBN-10: 0692467122

"Crimson and Clover" by Carly Berg first appeared in *Apocrypha and Abstractions*, March, 2013

"Night Eyes" by Bruce Boston first appeared in *Dark Wisdom*, January, 2005

"Heart of Steel" first appeared on *Every Day Fiction*, Episode 165, March 13, 2014

In This Issue

Spilt Blood, Sipped Honey

Samantha Kymmell-Harvey

Lucy crawled through the cornfield of mud and gore. She searched the pockets of her stolen Union uniform for a handkerchief, or anything to wipe the blood away. All she found was hard tack and matches. Shivering, she cursed herself for not checking the corpse's supplies before she had stripped him. There was no time, not when Joshua was still out there. She touched a hand gingerly to her belly. "We'll find your Papa," she said. "I promise."

The bloated bodies lay where they'd charged in straight lines, just like the cornrows they'd been killed in. Chewing her lip, Lucy examined each contorted face — none of them her Joshua.

As she stepped over a slumped body, something rolled under her foot tripping her. What broke her fall was too soft to be earth. Turning, she found a rebel body beneath her, headless, his bloody stump of a leg still snagged between her boots. Unable to suppress the burning gag at the back of her throat, she vomited.

The shredded cornhusks still smoldered around her, singeing the edges of her woolen cap. The battle had begun at dawn. Now, at dusk, only the campfires of bivouacs lit up the field. And from the silence of ceasefire came a low hum, as if the Earth itself vibrated a requiem. Lucy stopped and laid her hand against the chest of the corpse behind her. Something pinged against his ribs, buzzing. His gut wound no longer pulsed red, but amber. His soul had awakened, his blood now honey for the Keepers. They were coming.

"Joshua!" Lucy shrieked as a cloud of Keepers appeared on the horizon, their black cloaks flapping like wings. Lucy gazed out at the countless of dead fathers, sons, and brothers who would be Honeyed with no ceremony.

These dead would never be celebrated with a wake, nor laid upon white altars in the churchyard for their Keepers to come. No, these souls would be carried to Sweet Rest by the Keepers without their families even knowing they'd been killed. Nameless Honeying, – Lucy shivered – Not my Joshua. The buzzing corpses grew louder, calling to their collectors as the Keepers descended. Panic pulsed through Lucy's body as she darted through the field.

That morning she had watched Joshua's regimental colors march through the rows of corn from the hayloft of a barn. Below her, in the empty goat pens, surgeons amputated limbs. Nurses dumped wagons full of them into the Antietam Creek which flowed just beside them. Its waters ran scarlet from the chunks of flesh bobbing on the ripples. The snapping of bones echoed the rifle fire outside. The soldiers' shrieks masked Lucy's when she saw those regimentals colors fall.

Lucy neared the field's edge beside the road where she'd last seen his flag. Something dark swooped down just ahead of her. Lucy retreated, crouching behind bent cornstalks. The creature stood upright and walked as if through water. Lucy had never seen a Keeper before. When her granddaddy died, she'd wanted to hold his hand during the Honeying, but Mama said that the Honeying is between a soul and his Keeper.

Lucy pulled her cap low and watched. The Keeper pushed the hood of its cape down revealing a woman's face, paper gray, thin lips scarlet. Long black hair hung tangled like rotted corn silk against her back. On her skeletal arm hung a bee skep. Lucy only recognized it because her granddaddy had kept bees. Keepers collected souls in a skep.

The Keeper knelt beside the corpse, her eyes glistening amber in the setting sun. She unhooked the skep from her wrist. From her belt, she drew a thin silver dagger. Lucy crawled closer as the Keeper dragged the blade along the soldier's coat, buttons dropping into the blood-soaked mud. She then slashed his shirt to reveal his pale chest. Like a surgeon, she carved just under his ribs. His decaying skin split. The scent of rot permeated the air. Lucy swallowed, thinking she might retch again. A bee, glistening wet with blood-honey, emerged and flew into the Keeper's skep. Then she lowered herself and put her lips to the pulsing golden liquid.

Lucy bit her hand to keep from screaming. Turning her face away, she placed a hand on her belly. Not her husband. Not her child. A sharp kick thumped against her hand as if to agree. Lucy lifted her head. Her eyes fixed on the darkness beyond the creature. Onwards.

She padded softly by the Keeper as it ate. Nearing the road, Lucy saw a man in Federal uniform lying on his side, head propped up against another corpse, also clad in blue. She knelt beside him. A pale face, darkened from soot, looked back at her. Joshua.

"You with the medical corps? I'm gut shot," Joshua said.

Lucy half-smiled. He didn't recognize her. "It's me, my love." She removed her cap. Her dark braid tumbled over her shoulder. "I've come to take you home."

Joshua grasped her fingers, pinching them, rubbing his blood between them. The flecks of bone were like grit against her skin. "You are not my Lucy."

"Hush now, I'm here." she as she placed a hand against his abdomen. His blood seeped warmly. The hole in his woolen waistcoat was perfectly round. Gulping back tears, she knew his wound was mortal.

"Go." A thin rivulet of dark ruby liquid, tinged with amber, trickled from the corner of Joshua's lips. Lucy wiped it with her sleeve. His blood had started to turn. "I don't want you to see me like that."

Lucy hugged him to her chest, smearing his blood-honey across her cheek. "They can't have you. We both have something to live for." She took his hand and pressed it against her abdomen. He smiled weakly and squeezed her fingers. He knew now. And as she kissed his forehead, she felt his hand slip, his breath sputtering before he exhaled for the final time. His eyes, open, fixed on hers. Lucy laid her head on his chest, and cried.

The screams of the dying and the buzzing of the dead deafened Lucy. Goose bumps sprouted on her arms. The scent of sulfurous rot permeated the breeze.

"Go," said a voice, strong and rich and sweet. "You should not be here."

Lucy lifted her head defiantly. The Keeper hovered over her. The creature's corpse-like face was no longer gray. Her ruby lips glistened, sticky with honey, her pale cheeks now rosy from drinking life force away. Her amber eyes blazed.

"You cannot take him like this." Lucy clung to Joshua.

"This is death," she said. "Your ceremonies do not change the borders between your world and mine."

As Lucy hugged her husband, she felt his bee-soul throbbing against her chest. "Joshua, forgive me," she whispered to him.

"It calls to me," said the Keeper. "You would not deprive your loved one of the Sweet Rest, would you?"

Lucy held her head up. "No, it is not his time. He is to be a father. We've wanted this for so long." She ran a hand over her own belly. "He *will* meet his child."

"You cannot deny death. To do so is only selfish," said the Keeper. "Go home, love your child dearly, and I will come for you when it is your time."

The Keeper plucked Joshua from Lucy and lowered his body between the smoldering cornstalks.

"Stop!" Lucy waded through honey-soaked limbs, decapitated heads oozing blood-honey from their open mouths. Bones crackled and poked her toes through her boots. The hem of her trousers clung to her legs, sticky.

The Keeper bent over Joshua, silver dagger ready. Lucy heard a pop. Her stomach roiled at the sound of Joshua's flesh splitting. Lucy screamed, lunging at the Keeper. She turned and pushed Lucy down, leaving honeyed handprints on her shoulders.

And as the Keeper lowered her lips to Joshua's blood-honey, a small black thing buzzed, zipping round her then crawled inside the straw skep. The Keeper had reaped his soul.

"No!" Lucy leaped over the Keeper, snagged the skep, and ran.

Lucy's thoughts raced as she sprinted. The Keeper's cloak slapped behind her in the wind. She needed to free Joshua's bee-soul before the Keeper caught her. How did granddaddy retrieve the honey from the comb? He'd light a fire and when the smoke surrounded the hive, the bees fled. She knew what she needed. *Smoke.*

Lucy fumbled to retrieve the matches from her pocket. As she struck it, a flame finally ignited. But a cold gust rushed over her, extinguishing the flame. The Keeper had descended.

"There will be two more souls to reap tonight if you do not give me my skep." The Keeper pointed a jagged finger at Lucy's belly.

Lucy hugged the skep against her stomach protectively. The Keeper pinned her gray foot against Lucy's leg and yanked the skep away. But as the creature began to take flight, Lucy struck another match. The flames rushed up the cornstalk singeing the Keeper's cloak. The creature howled, dropping the skep. Lucy grabbed it and retreated behind the thickening veil of smoke.

Plodding through the corn, Lucy watched as Joshua's bee-soul cautiously emerged, still wet with blood-honey. She trapped him in her hands.

Shouts of the living rose from the field as the crackling fire spread. Lucy sprinted back to Joshua's body, skep hanging from her wrist. His prickly bee-soul bounced against her fingers. The Keeper huffed and screeched behind her, searching.

Joshua's body lay where the Keeper had abandoned him. Blood-honey still pulsed from his chest. The creature hadn't finished drinking. If enough remained, then perhaps she could return his life force with the blood-honey inside the skep. Lucy's heart seized her throat.

But as she knelt, skeletal fingers jabbed into her spine, pushing her from behind. Lucy screamed and tumbled into the honey-tainted mud beside Joshua's body. A sharp pain seared through her hand. Opening her fingers, she saw a bright red welt on the heel of her palm. Joshua had stung her. Lucy cupped him in her other hand.

The Keeper stood over her. "He has tasted Sweet Rest. He will not be the same as you remember," said the Keeper.

Lucy shook her head. "You're lying." Her palm throbbed as if on fire. Unable to fight the pain any longer, she brought the welt to her lips and sucked.

The taste of sweet blood-honey seeped into her tongue. She closed her eyes, succumbing to the ecstasy. The syrup was smooth and sweet, like drinking in wildflowers. It spread hot through her veins, bringing sweat to her brow. A great thirst ached in her throat. She sucked her palm again, but there was no more honey.

"You foolish girl," said the Keeper. "To drink my nourishment." The creature lunged, bearing her black, decaying teeth.

The Keeper's cold nails dug into Lucy's thin skin as they both clasped the skep. The smoke grew thick around them, fire licking at their feet. Lucy stood over Joshua, struggling to force the creature back. The straw crackled as it split. The Keeper flew up, half the skep in her arms. Lucy fell back, gripping the other half. The blood-honey dripped down her hands. The rest pooled on Joshua's body. The smell of it made Lucy's mouth water. She clenched her jaw, fighting the urge to drink as she gently placed Joshua's bee-soul into his abdomen.

Joshua's blood shimmered, changing from golden to copper to scarlet as his flesh received its life force again. His ashen skin flushed pink. Joshua groaned and gasped, his back arching.

"It is done," said the Keeper, stealing her skep from Lucy's grasp. "He will live. But the thirst will never leave you."

Tears welling in Lucy's eyes, she shook her hands as if to rid them of the blood, honey, and mud. "What am I?"

The Keeper's black eyes were piercing. "Not one of us. Just a soul stranded between the worlds." Her cloak flapped in the wind, smoke dispersing, flames dying.

Lucy screamed.

The baby's cries woke Lucy. She lit the tallow candle to find Joshua rocking in his chair. He stared out the window, blue eyes fixed on something Lucy couldn't see.

"Aren't you going to comfort your daughter?" Lucy laid a hand on his shoulder. He didn't look at her.

"I hear them buzzing in the field," he said. "Do you?"

Lucy swallowed, pushing the regret from her mind. They were a family. "You were just having a nightmare," she said. "You're home. You're safe."

Joshua turned, mouth agape. "But I hear them. Always."

Lucy's mouth watered, her tongue longing for the honey she'd been dreaming of. *If this is what you call alive,* she thought as she scooped the baby up from her crib. "Hush, sweet girl. We'll both eat."

Lucy ran a hand along her daughter's soft gray skin. Her eyes glistened amber in the candlelight. Lucy draped a small bonnet to hide them. "I'm sorry," Lucy whispered as she opened the cupboard. Pushing aside the jars of salted meats and preserves, she clasped the earthenware pot. Nestled together, Lucy dipped her finger in the glimmering blood-honey. The baby grabbed it, jammed it between her scarlet lips, and sucked happily. Lucy's eyes drifted to the church steeple on the horizon as the bells chimed two. She shivered. Tomorrow would be another Honeying. Tomorrow, her jar would be full.

Samantha Kymmell-Harvey's *stories can be found in* Waylines Magazine, Spark: A Creative Anthology, *and* Every Day Fiction *just to name a few. She is a 2012 graduate of the* Odyssey Writing Workshop. *You can follow her on her blog:* http://samanthakymmell-harvey.blogspot.com

No Madonna

Marge Simon

At sunset she serves herself,
a candle on the breakfast tray,
a glass of wine, a plate of fruit.

She flips through an album as she eats,
her trials and loves in photographs
her life a maze of various threads;

a damask tablecloth from Surrey,
embroidered towels, silver spoons
that green silk dress, a size too small
she wore for King Henry's ball.

Melmac dishes from the sixties
the kind a gypsy could afford
and never broke when thrown.

The dark haired boy with smoky eyes,
she made him happy for a time,
until her needs got in the way.
A shredded ticket to Belize.

Sven, who never understood a word
but never did that matter, at the time.
One last sleigh ride in the snowy hills.
Green yarn from a knitted hat.

That sad faced man with the cowboy hat,
and the older gentleman, the one she wed,
both cattlemen and rich, back in the day.
A columbine, pressed in wax paper.

The lady smiles,
having absorbed them all
into her many passions.

She blots her lips, wipes her fangs
with a clean blue napkin.

Marge Simon's *works appear in publications such as* Strange Horizons,
Niteblade, DailySF Magazine, Pedestal Magazine, Dreams & Night-
mares. *She edits a column for the HWA Newsletter and serves as Chair of
the Board of Trustees. She has won the Strange Horizons Readers Choice
Award, the Bram Stoker Award™(2008, 2012, 2013), the Rhysling Award
and the Dwarf Stars Award. Collections:* Like Birds in the Rain, Unearthly
Delights, The Mad Hattery, Vampires, Zombies & Wanton Souls, *and*
Dangerous Dreams. Member HWA, SFWA, SFPA. *www.margesimon.com*

CRIMSON AND CLOVER

Carly Berg

Baby hair stuck up through the mulch, feathery blond tufts, *dammit*. Millie tossed her rose clippers down and yanked him out of the ground like a turnip. The boy remained still and gray even after the mud was scooped from his mouth. But when she snipped the roots, freeing the carcass for the trash can, he howled like a storm.

In the kitchen, the greedy thing drank half a bottle of liquid houseplant food from the dropper.

She lay him in an inch of water in the sink to keep him moist. He kicked his twiggy legs.

"Bring me a big flowerpot, would you?" she called to Jack, since by then she was thawing ground beef in the pan.

"Christ on a cracker, Millie. Not another one."

"What do you want me to do about it?" she asked. She'd told him the place was built on the old Woodstock field but he just had to have it anyway.

"Dirty hippies," he said as if reading her mind.

"You got that right. See if there's any more potting soil out there too, would ya?"

Jack potted the new dirt baby while Millie fixed Hamburger Helper.

Late nights, they sneak a few babies onto the neighbors' porches.

They awake to a few of the neighbors' babies on theirs.

The little ones need their soil changed often and to be fed by hand. The older ones hop around the garden nibbling the plants down to nubs with their lipless mouths. They howl when they're hungry. They're always hungry. They give no love. It's all me, me, me.

Carly Berg *gets her three hots and a cot near Houston. Her collection of flash* stories, Coffee House Lies, *is available at Amazon.com.*

IN THE STONE GARDEN *by Midas*

∽✠∾

A twenty-seven year old photographer going by his nickname of **Midas,**
opened a studio in 1995 with a goal, to establish a presence in a tiny town
where no studios existed. He envisioned a place where up and coming models
could develop their portfolios without driving two hours to the nearest city.
And to see these models published in print either in ads or articles However
in small towns, the talent was scarce and most clients were content with stay-
ing home. After a few years without getting a model established and published and with pressure from his fiancé; **Midas** closed the doors, sold his
cameras and studio equipment and rode west to Tennessee with his soon to be
wife.

Still the idea left behind in small town Virginia never left **Midas.** Now mar-
ried and with a child, a subject would catch his eye and could picture the per-
son in a pictorial. However with no camera in his possession, he would never
see his visions come to life.

In 2011, it wasn't much but his family bought him a small point and shoot
digital camera and the following year **Midas** decided to step back into the
photography world. And by 2012, social networking opened doors which never existed and he found subjects which became new clients. And by early
2014, he began to work with established models and helped to open doors into
publishing.

Within four months, **Midas'** work and models have been featured in ten publications. All this with no fancy cameras and no studio just using a camera,
flash, and laptop. **Midas** is uncertain what will happen in 2015 but he is sure
the 27 year old in a small town would be green with envy.

Hate

Florence Grey

Hate is a hard thing.
Its edges are sharp and jagged, and you
Don't really notice it too much, until it's too late—
And it cuts you, marks your skin leaving its dark
Impression forever.
No matter how much time passes, the edges never dull.
It is efficient.
It's a drug in some aspects, easily triggered, and easily found.
Hate is nourished by anger fed by greed, and fostered in the
Ideology of pride now wronged.
Hate festers just under the surface of scars and wounds that
Just won't ever die, and that the mind cannot forget.
The bitter saltiness of raw unsettled reality, its sobering after effects.
Fiery pain from its formidable touch, we are all masochists underneath—
Too soon we forget its piercing claws, too slow we are to see it coming.

Florence Grey *has been writing poetry for nearly twenty years. She loves the swing and big band era and prefers writing her poetry with pen and paper to that of a computer.*

Religious Artifacts

Luiz H. Coelho

The ancient walls shook with the drill's vibration; a large hole was being made on the ceiling. A round portion of the roof fell to the dusty ground with a loud crash. The two archaeologists dropped down with a zip line, both in highly-advanced protective suits. It was forty degrees below zero outside, and an ice-storm was on its way. The wind howled ferociously, and a few snowflakes dropped down in the halo of light under the hole.

"Outstanding, Geff!" cried the older scientist, removing his domed helmet.

Around them were half a dozen preserved skeletons, trapped long ago in these cavernous ruins. The structure had remained concealed and untouched for ages. There were rows of what appeared to be shelves, with volumes of long-forgotten lore from a more primitive time.

"What do you think this place is supposed to be, Mr. Fenn?" questioned the younger researcher, who was examining one of the dusty volumes.

"It seems to be some sort of library of religious texts," answered the more experienced Fenn as he dusted off what seemed to be an image, crudely pasted upon the wall and worn away by time.

It was a very realistic depiction of an extremely well-built figure in ritualistic colorful robes imposingly standing against the sky. This place must have been some form of temple.

"Look at this!" cried Geff, excited, as he skimmed through one of the supposed religious texts.

There were crude depictions of exaggerated deities doing battle, without any semblance of a narrative. Strange markings surrounded the action. There were thousands of these slim volumes, some scattered on the floor but most neatly packed in the old wooden shelves.

"Let's take one of these. Maybe someone up top will be able to translate them. Who knows what they're worth," suggested Fenn as he removed another copy from the hands of one of the skeletons, who had been clutching at it in fetal position.

"They always turn to religion when things go awry. Didn't do him any good, though. I'm guessing this place is at least a few centuries old," pondered the wiser archeologist.

The younger scientist looked at one of the corpses. "Oh...It's a child," he exclaimed. In its hand was a small carved statue. It appeared to be a dark humanoid figure with a horned head. It bore some resemblance to a certain flying mammal, one that was now extinct. Early religions tended to have anthropomorphized deities.

"I guess they were indoctrinated from a very young age. What's this?" He got closer to the juvenile skeleton, and turned the diminutive skull, making it face him.

There were numerous rows of miniscule metallic structures around the dead child's teeth; they appeared to have been quite painful in life. It wasn't the only corpse with such devices in its oral cavities.

"This must be some sort of primitive torture device, Mr. Fenn," He nervously exclaimed.

"I wouldn't be surprised. They seem quite primitive. Look at this," responded his older partner, as he handed his colleague a peculiar yellow object. It was reminiscent of a small wooden dagger, ending in a sharp point.

"It couldn't have been used for hunting. The point breaks too easily; though it may be poisonous," commented the elder of the two researchers, perplexed.

They moved towards a small table with some kind of rudimentary map with miniature warriors on it. There were other strange objects with curious geometrical shapes and indecipherable sigils upon them as well.

"They might have been preparing for battle. This could have been a religious haven during the Great War. Perhaps they were not as primitive as we think. Try translating some of the markings, Geff, this could be a big discovery," Suggested Fenn, excitedly dusting off more skeletons.

Geff examined a large machine on a table by the wall. Black boxes surrounded it, and there were many indentations and nobs. He pressed one of them, and the archeologists were surprised with a choir of religious chanting, emanating from the boxes. It was extremely loud, and the vibrations raised another cloud of dust. Tribal drums were heard, and then unintelligible incantations. After a few seconds, the boxes were silent once more, and smoke began to rise from them.

"Damn it, Geff! Have you finished translating yet?" The dizzied researcher bitterly asked his partner, who was cleaning off a large corroded sign near what appeared to be the exit to the buried temple.

"I'm almost done with this, I think. It's something regarding mythical creatures and caverns or prisons," responded Geff, embarrassed.

"We should get going. Find something you think might be valuable and let's get out of here before the storm locks us in with these corpses. This place gives me the creeps," commented the elder.

His youthful partner nodded in agreement as he picked up the rusty sign from the floor. The writing on it was dusty and still appeared to be indecipherable.

Both scientists ascended the zip line with their findings in clear bags, and marked the locale with a colored flag on the snowy surface. As they headed back to base on their automatic transport, Geff proceeded to turn on his portable music device, and put miniature speakers in his ears as he unfolded an illustrated scroll to read at his leisure. Mr. Fenn smiled condescendingly and uttered: "We've sure come a long way."

The sign at the entrance was eventually translated by a team of linguists as "Lloyd's Comics". The words baffled scholars and explorers alike, ensuring that the temple's true nature would remain a mystery, lost to the ages.

Luiz H. Coelho *is a Brazilian-Canadian Film Student that dabbles in writing whenever his schedule allows it. If you enjoyed his story (which he hopes you did), you can read more about him* at
www.EpicClubBlog.blogspot.com

QUILTING

JD DeHart

It was a magic Appalachian art form
The evidence of craft still hanging
Off the beaten path of the highways
The centers for the arts are still around
Go in, discover the mugs, napkin rings
Dolls made of cornhusk, diverse items

Do not miss the marigold one
It appears there are stains
This one is of particular interest
There is a companion narrative

Kathy came from the unlatched screen door
World of the mountains, where all gossip
Was beat out into the wind like sheets
She bathed in the river and ate from vines

When Kathy fell in love, and the thief girl
Stole the beau, he wound up wrapped
In the fabric; sure, he appears a stag
Antlers broad, but the bewildered look
Tells you a story of charming surprise
Never expecting to be part of the fabric
No one knows what became of the thief –
One of the dolls bears her marks
With the same expression of shock.

JD DeHart *is a writer and teacher. His short collection,* The Truth About Snails, *is available on Amazon.*

WULVER OF THE HIGHLANDS

Kyle Newton

It knew to strike after all torchlight faded. Unnatural speed and agility moved the creature through trees and brambles. The beast stilled as it stood upon a large rock jutting from the hill. A breeze from the Loch brought a cold warning to remain inside. But, not all obeyed. A full moon cast its spotlight, masking everything in a white hue. Gilt eyes fell upon the village. Its next victim. Claws scratched against rock. A long nose twitched, hoping to find the scent of anyone who may have forgotten curfew. The predator's gray fur danced in the chilled air. Puffs of mist were seen as it panted. Pattering of young feet reached stiffened ears. With a grunt the monster charged downhill and into the settlement. A blood tribute must now be paid.

This small village sat alone atop the mountain. To avoid jagged and rough terrain, a single road guided travelers through it and over the Highland. Few ever used this lone trail, including traders. Most travelers, if any, came during the day. And for good reason.

Hunting here before, the creature entered with little distress. It stood on its hind legs, in search of what scent teased it from the hilltop. Too large for any door, the creature knew it needed to draw them out. Bloodshed had never failed before.

The beast stood motionless. Its pointed ears twitched, listening to everything within its hunting ground. Humans walking inside homes, often followed by a panting dog. Pets were easy prey, but never tasted good to this predator. Tonight, it salivated for the crunch of human bones. A contracting nose guided the head and eyes as it shuffled through different scents. Muscles on its upper arms flexed and relaxed upon hearing movement. The hunter scratched at the ground with clawed toes, growing in excitement. Excitement dared it to strike early.

A dim light shined as a door opened four houses away. The creature's eyes found a young lad stepping outside. Before attacking, it watched to see if the boy noticed. Whether he did not see this hunter or did not care, the child stood there and gave three sharp whistles.

"C'mere puppy," the boy whispered.

A snarl climbed up the monster's snout: saliva slid down every razor-sharp tooth. No longer interested in the boy's foolishness, the creature raced toward its next victim, galloping on all fours. With each pound on the ground its demonic speed increased. Three large steps and a lunge were all its jaws needed to claim their bloody trophy. The unfortunate lad never saw its approach.

Familiar and foreign faces alike filled the tavern. Vegetable soup and ale plugged everyone's nostrils as song and laughter danced in their ears. A man carrying a small tabor drum encouraged the music to continue. A local drunk known as McAllister, had already passed out in a dim-lit corner. The tavern: *The Broken Antler* fit forty Scotsman comfortably. Tonight looked more like fifty. Anice, a young fair-haired woman and the tavern's sole barmaid, scratched her fingernails against a wooden table as their rowdiness grew. Her small, round face snarled as mugs of ale splashed everywhere.

This wooden structure held eight tables and a bar spanning the far wall. Crackling flames sat in a fireplace to its right. To the bar's left were animal pelts. Above all of these furs sat a pair of antlers with one side broken, about half the length of its counterpart. Four timber support-columns stretched to the ceiling. Being in a small town not far from Loch Ness, *The Broken Antler* had always been a last stop for travelers before trudging up the mountain's lonely dirt way.

Most patrons were easygoing — as far as a group of clansmen can be crowded so close together. The bard started to play his favorite tune when screams and wailing silenced him. Soon, everyone followed the bard in his stillness as a second voice echoed.

"Help! Please, someone help us!" Two men came crashing through the tavern's door. Everyone in the tavern leapt to their feet, except McAllister, who drooled in a drunken slumber. As barstools toppled over, the sea of patrons shivered with what they saw. Blood and sweat matted long hair around one man's forehead. A bald and much taller man followed. His clothing: riddled with small tears and cuts. His ashen pallor matched his wide, unblinking eyes.

"You must help us!" The tall man continued to cry out. Fatigue dropped him to his knees.

Shoving two Scotsmen away, a kind patron ran to his aid. He rested a hand on the back of the man's head, keeping him propped up.

"Grab somethin' he can rest his head on!" The patron shouted to the crowd. He noticed a familiar red, blue, and green tartan on both men's kilts: often worn by Murray clansman.

"You two come from the mountain don't ya?" The injured man nodded as his new friend used a sleeve to wipe away some of the blood. "Don't ya worry friend, ye're safe now."

Softness in his words brought the injured man to a weep.

"It took my s-son. My son is...gone," he sobbed.

Anice elbowed her way through ranks of Scotsmen with rolled blankets under each arm and a mug of water in hand. She handed her drink over before watching the bald man's dry throat cough up any water that passed his lips. His second attempt at taking a sip proved far more successful.

"Who took your son?" Anice asked.

"Our village came under attack," the long-haired man answered. "Last night—it came out of the woods. It-it took Davey's son first."

"What beast came from the woods? Bears?" another patron asked.

"N-no, not...not a bear." Davey struggled, rising to his knees. He found a wooden chair next to his friend and sat down with him. "It wa-was *the White Wolf*," he answered through heavy pants. "It took my family from me." Davey covered his face with one hand and slammed the other against a table.

Whispers of a *White Wolf* passed through the tavern like spiders. Most had never heard of such a creature.

"There ain't no wolves in d'ese parts," one man said. "It couldn't have been a wolf."

"This ain't no regular wolf, laddie. They be speakin' of a special type of wolf. Ain't ye?" An older man stepped around the bar and approached both Murrays. White strands speckled his black hair and beard. He wore a faded blue shirt underneath his blue and green plaid great-kilt. The unmistakable Forbes tartan.

The two Murrays looked at each other, then to the old man and nodded their heads.

"James and I thought no one would believe us when we told 'em," Davey said. "You know of this creature?"

"Aye. I've seen the beast wit' ma own eyes lad." Scowls from patrons found the old man. His nightly tales of fable and myth were unwanted at such a time.

"You and all yer tall tales father," the barmaid snapped. "If *Angus: The Great Hunter* had seen it, the skin would be on yer tavern wall."

"That be one beast I will never kill," Angus answered.

"Never kill it? It took my family!" Dave rose to his feet. "I say we go find and kill the animal!"

A loud roar of agreeing tavern patrons brought a shiver to the *Broken Antler's* foundation. Everyone gave a hardy cheer as Angus hung his head. James alone took note of this. The wary stranger quieted his friend, then approached Angus.

"You know somethin', don't ya?" He asked. His questioned summoned a silence amongst the patrons. The Murray clansman gritted his teeth. "Please, sir. You've got to help us."

Angus shook his head. His stare met James.

"It ain't 'cause I don't want to help ya, lad," he stated. "It's 'cause I already tried. I've seen what this creature can do ta' folks. I wish the beast didn't go after yer family. But this is something I won't be helpin' ya wit'."

"I beg of you," Davey pleaded. "It killed my family. I'm lucky to have gotten here alive! The Forbes and Murray clans were once brought together by Carl the Short. Do not let his hard work go unnoticed 'ere."

Angus looked to the large man—their eyes met. Davey's glassy expression made him hesitate to answer.

"Sit here, Davey." Angus approached the two men and found a seat next to them. "Now, I won't be going out there, helpin' ya kill this beast. But I can tell ya what ya face. It happened two winters ago, not far from Drumnadrochit."

☙✠❧

"Lawrence...where is everyone?" Angus yelled to his friend through heavy breaths. Sweat cascaded down his forehead.

Lawrence's curled, fiery hair matted itself all around his long face. Blood trickled down the corner of his mouth. A man with short black hair wearing the same green and white plaid kilt followed close behind.

"The creature found us, Angus," his friend screamed. "We were lookin' for you and your kin and it chased us down. After we were separated from you, we heard screams and feared the worst." Lawrence rested—hands atop his knees—for a much needed breather. "Where-where's your kin?" he asked. As Lawrence realized who remained, raw nerves pulled at his stomach.

Angus shook his head. A tear ran down his cheek. Silence said everything. Lawrence placed a hand on his mourning friend's shoulder. His jaw stiffened as a scowl formed.

"We'll kill the bast'd yet," he said.

A snapping of twigs interrupted the inspiring moment. Lawrence's brother spun around to face the woods they were trapped in.

"Lawrence! It found us again!" Never being much in the way of a warrior, Lawrence's little brother wielded two small dirks. The older brother possessed a basket-hilted long sword. Angus's sword had been lost in his last standoff with the beast. Leaving him with a rake he found alongside a fallen clansman. Each stood with their back to the other two.

"Be sharp, lads!" Angus demanded. "If we attack this together we can still kill it!" Callused hands wrapped around his rake.

Grunts echoed through trees while the ground shook from the creature's pounding feet. Angus's breaths fell in cadence with galloping legs.

Lawrence scanned through trees. Shadows teased the corner of his eyes. Before his sight focused, the forest fell silent. All three Scotsmen glanced at one another. Whitened knuckles revealed none choose to flee.

Before anyone spoke, a cluster of small trees splintered in all directions. A large beast covered in white fur leaped through wooden fragments and slammed to the ground. When it stood, the monster towered over all three men. Terror chilled the spine of each Scot— none felt the strength to attack. The wolf glared at them with narrowed gilt eyes. A curled lip showed the creature found a sense of enjoyment in the fear that possessed its prey.

Angus knew he had to do something. With reckless abandon, he charged the animal. It took half a step back. Uncommon bravery for such prey. Paying for its mistake, slashes of a rake found their mark on the wolf's furry chest, ending at its stomach.

The beast swung a powerful arm at Angus, knocking him off his feet. He remained motionless upon landing, keeping his eyes closed. This Scotsman had been through enough fights to know when they had ended.

"The worst feeling in the world is hearing ya best friend scream for his life and there's not a thing ye can do for him." As Angus finished his story, he didn't look up from the floor.

James put a hand on Angus' back. A familiar scowl formed.

"I thank you for your tale and am sorry for yer loss. No one blames you for what ya did. We all would'a done the same." He pointed to the crowd in the tavern. "But we have more people than you did. It attacked my village. It killed Davey's family. We're going to get our revenge." He turned to the rest of the tavern. "Who's wit' me?"

With clenched fists raised, another loud cheer shook the tavern. This time, their battle-cry awoke McAllister. It didn't take long before Davey and James rallied everyone out the door and up to their village. Once the tavern emptied—leaving he and Anice alone, Angus took a deep breath. He approached one of his shutters. Pushing both sides open revealed a mob of vengeful villagers fading into an endless night.

"Ya know I'm going to follow 'em, don't ya father?"

"Was yer hunger that bad t'night?" he asked. Angus did not wish to see the glimmer in Anice's eyes.

"Aye. It took everything I had not to take them all here. I almost lost control after smelling the bald one's blood." The bar maiden rested on a shifted hip. "Oh, and telling them *you* swung the rake: very creative."

"I had to—for yer sake." He turned to his daughter. "Yer cravings have been gettin' worse by the day! They've made ya reckless!"

"And what would you have me do? Lose me mind? Mother tried that if ya don't remember!" Angus looked to the wooden floor. A quick step from Anice demanded his stare remain on her. "Well? What would you have me do?" Her voice echoed through an empty tavern. Angus gave a glance back into the night. A stillness hung in the air, waiting for the return of its cherished predator.

"They're already climbing up the hill."

"Shall I?" Her beautiful green eyes formed a gilt trim. No other option remained. He loved his daughter but feared what lay within her. Angus sat at a table where a full mug of ale still lingered.

"Take the back door—don't let anyone see ya. And for God's sake finish your work this time. I'm tired of cleanin' up after ya."

Anice looked to the dying fire as her irises were veiled in gold. Taking a step towards the back door, she hunched over in pain, grabbing her stomach. Returning to a full stand, muscles tightened as her body flexed. A small tear in the brown-stained blouse showed three large scratches defacing her stomach. Anice's breathing turned into slow and deep grunts.

Angus took a sip of ale as he heard his back door slam shut. A howled echoed. He had heard it countless times before, yet a quiver still claimed his body. The White Wolf had been freed.

Already familiar with how such tales end, Angus wondered when his daughter might befall the same fate of her mother and be found at the edge of a clansman's sword. Hoping that it not be tonight, he took another long swig of ale and prepared to join his fellow villagers. Similar to Lawrence, the barkeep wanted to make the villager's think he fought alongside them. Friendship has always been good for a final thought amongst dying men. And at least his conscience rested easier, knowing he gave them that.

Two books and multiple short stories published, the New England *born* Kyle Newton *has been found to merge fantasy and sci-fi with a macabre twist of letting few characters survive his tales. With local actors and directors, he's currently set his sights on bringing this style to the silver screen.*

In a Different Time and Place, It could have been Love, but Instead...

J. J. Steinfeld

How late in life they met
romantic broken like branches
in an indifferent storm
too many harsh winters
and less than satisfying summers
both with drinks in hand
"I have a mountain of regrets,"
she said, looking upward,
"I have an ocean of regrets,"
he said, looking downward
she had a gun, he a knife,
a bad film noir, certainly,
but in a different time and place
it could have been love
but instead they exchanged weapons
laughed about regrets
drank even more
words tumbled out of their thoughts
there was lovemaking
there was senseless talk of a future

the past kept intruding
like those harsh winters
and less than satisfying summers
one almost smiled
the other cried
each became the other's past.

The jury, if dark truth be told,
had little sympathy
for the victim or the other.

Canadian fiction writer, poet, and playwright J. J. Steinfeld *lives on Prince Edward Island, where he is patiently waiting for Godot's arrival and a phone call from Kafka. While waiting, he has published fifteen books, including* Disturbing Identities *(Stories, Ekstasis Editions),* Should the Word Hell Be Capitalized? *(Stories, Gaspereau Press),* Would You Hide Me? *(Stories, Gaspereau Press),* An Affection for Precipices *(Poetry, Serengeti Press),* Misshapenness *(Poetry, Ekstasis Editions),* Word Burials *(Novel and Stories, Crossing Chaos Enigmatic Ink),* A Glass Shard and Memory *(Stories, Recliner Books), and* Identity Dreams and Memory Sounds *(Poetry, Ekstasis Editions). More than three-hundred of his short stories and seven-hundred poems have appeared in anthologies and periodicals internationally, and over forty of his one-act plays and a handful of full-length plays have been performed in Canada and the United States.*

Night Eyes

Bruce Boston

From my seat at a corner table I watched her laughing and chatting at the bar, crossing and uncrossing her legs on the high stool. Her eyes never met mine though I saw them flash across the room more than once with sparks of light like tiny knives...and I wondered at the source of that illumination. For there was no light that sharp for her eyes to reflect.

I was in some nameless bar on some nameless street in the city. There are always plenty of bars on any street here. I had been drinking for several hours and forgotten how I had arrived or what I hoped to find. The legs of the table where I sat were uneven. Or perhaps it was the floor beneath. Every time I rested my arm on the scarred surface of the wood, the table rocked one way. When I raised it, back the other. The dark liquid in my glass tilted this way and that.

Candles burned at several tables, their narrow flames vanishing and rising like specters as the anonymous patrons around me shifted in their chairs. The room was draped with sheets of smoke gathering one atop another. The dusty globes over the bar gave off a pale blue radiance that revealed little of the scene beyond. There was no source of light bright enough for her eyes to catch and reflect...though there it was again, that dagger sharp flash cast in another direction than mine. The rest of her remained in shadow. Her features were vague, her body a shifting silhouette.

Naturally I took this as a sign.

When she left by herself I followed. There is always someone to follow in the city. Someone alone in the night.

She slipped quickly into the dark streets. My body felt thick and my limbs heavy as I moved after her. The streets of the city run every which way. There are countless cul-de-sacs. There are passages where one must enter unlit tunnels to cross beneath the lighted thorough-fares above. Places where darkness gathers more deeply than is natural.

It was just as easy to lose someone in this unplanned maze as to catch them. Easy to become lost oneself. Rumor has it these streets are haunted by those who have never returned from some solitary midnight errand or evening stroll. I believe I had met more than one of those lost souls in my own nocturnal jaunts. I had played with the idea that I might be such a deserted creature myself.

The night was dark as usual. Many of the streetlights in this district were broken or unlit. Others flickered wanly like dying strobes, casting the squares and buildings in serial snapshots of varying intensity. Overhead a partial moon was occluded by a rind of clouds. The stars were invisible beyond the overcast.

Her retreating form mingled with the night, her jacket and pants often no more than a smudge of lighter black against the deeper black that surrounded it, defined more by its movement than its shade. I thought for a moment I had lost her. I paused to listen for footsteps and there was only silence. Then she glanced back over her shoulder.

She stood motionless less than half a block away. Her eyes flared brighter than before with that same sharp cut of light, revealing her slender figure and the street around her. Only now they were turned in my direction. She knew she was being followed.

She looked away and moved on, though her steps were no faster. I imagined she was anticipating the closure of our embrace.

I trailed her down to the harbor district, where a sluggish estuary of the river backs up against the city, churning the same muddied waters in endless circles until a storm dissipates them and they form again.

Surely she could not live here. The hulking shapes of abandoned warehouses rose about us like the carcasses of scavenged beasts. I smelled the dank shoreline and the rotting wood of the pier. The pavement beneath my feet was slick with moisture, littered with broken glass and debris.

As we crossed from the pavement onto the sand of the beach, a sudden chill invaded my body and the damp air. I was close behind her now. I could hear her breath. I could almost reach out and touch the leather of her jacket, the trailing stands of her jet black hair. Yet when she suddenly turned to face me and meet my glance, I stopped short.

Her features and the expression upon them were revealed for the first time. I realized she was something other than human, and she no doubt thought the same of me.

I saw the light in her eyes full on, burning, skeletal and manic in the purity of its hard brilliance. I understood that it did not reflect any light in our surroundings, for there was only the night on all sides. Rather whoever or whatever she was had gathered and reflected the deepest fires that burned at the core of that night. For even the dark must have its flame to survive, its fuel to feed upon.

She took me by the arm, the one holding the knife, and led me down to the brackish waters. I could hear the low waves lapping against the shore, though I could not see them. All I could see were her eyes. I wondered if they would still glow once we were submerged. And if so, would their light be any softer?

Bruce Boston *is the author of more than fifty books and chapbooks, including the novels* The Guardener's Tale *and* Stained Glass Rain. *His writing has received the Bram Stoker Award, a Pushcart Prize, the Asimov's Readers Award, and the Grand Master Award of the Science Fiction Poetry Association.*

ILLUMINATED WEB *by Cynthia Staples*

Cynthia Staples *is a photographer and writer living in Somerville, MA. Through words and images, she tries to capture the beauty in the world around her. You can follow her creative journey at* wordsandimagesbycynthia.com.

Sunset in the Westerwald

Carl Grafe

Little Snow White,
Little Red Cap,
and Little Rose Thorn,
kinfolk-favored
and freely beloved,
their innocence bright
as the finest pearls
burning in the noonday sun

But the forest beckons,
and innocence and love
mist away like dreams
that die in der Nacht:
Schneewittchen, forsaken;
careless Rotkaeppchen;
and Dornroeschen, pricked
and a century slept

Each cold and allein
with cackling Hexen
and keen-eyed Zwerge,
hungriger Woelfe
und Dornenhecken,
Zauberformeln
und Geister und Monster
in der groesser dunkler Wald

Carl Grafe *lives with his family in the Salt Lake Valley, which he enjoys on days when it's not snowing. His short stories and poetry have appeared in* Star*Line, The Colored Lens, Perihelion Science Fiction, *and elsewhere.*

HEART OF STEEL

Jeremy Szal

I looked at myself in the mirror, wishing my eyes were lying to me — that this was all just some screwed up nightmare. But it wasn't. My eyes told the truth. My bony, pinkish arms were replaced with limbs that were gunmetal grey in colour, rimmed in by bolts and steel. Oxygen pumps and filtrations permitted me to continue breathing. Even when I touched my metal-clad torso I felt nothing. Nothing but the cold, dead metal that burned with loss and sorrow. Electrodes and cords replaced my blood and veins — the very things that sustained my body and kept me alive.

Am I dead?

Or was that just the human part of me that had disappeared into nothing, only to be replaced with a machine.

I clenched my fingers together to form an iron fist, feeling the tortured screech of scraping metal clashing against my palm. It sounded like I was in some sort of prison, hidden from the world outside. Is this what I was going to be like? My soul locked in a prison of tangled wires, coded programs, and a network of platinum and steel. What did I have left that was truly human?

Suddenly the anger bubbled inside me like hot oil. I smashed the mirror in front of me, shattering the nanocrystal glass. "You're the next step of our evolution as a species," they told me in hushed whispers. "The first of your kind. You represent the future of humanity."

It was a little hard to be part of humanity when I wasn't even human. I was on my own. An experiment. A scientific 'miracle'.

I picked up the datapad that detailed all the 'upgrades' by body had been given, careful not to shatter the pad. The words were clear, crisp and curt — like they had been stamped out by a printer with a mind of its own. It detailed how my bones had been re-enforced with density and fiber; how I had a neural device installed in my head, and the modification of my body tissue. Even my brain was now partially a machine. Could I really be called a human, when everything I had stored in my head, emotions, memories, feelings, thoughts—everything that defined who I was—had been replaced, muddled with, and transformed into something artificial?

How could I even be sure my memories were mine?

"That mirror was expensive," Lumen, my AI and long-suffering friend said. She made an exasperated sound as the bathroom camera zoomed in. "Why did you break it?"

"You damn well know why," I said. Lumen could see the rate of my artificial heart beating, the spiking radio signals of my neural-enhanced brain, and the oxygen I breathed in through my artificial lungs. She knew I was angry and why.

"The accident changed nothing," she said, "you're still human. You are who you make yourself to be. You aren't defined by society or body organs."

The sick irony of an artificial intelligence telling a cyborg about what defined a human being was almost funny. Lumen was a good friend and she wanted nothing but the best for me. Most AIs had their intellect levels capped on purchase and were treated as servants, referred to by a cluster of meaningless digits. I refused to see Lumen that way.

But at the same time I knew that I wasn't anything more than she was.

An artificial program.

A machine.

The accident had made sure of that. I couldn't even remember falling. All I could recall was the pain and how it burned and burned…eating away at me like acid. It took hours for them to find me, but they were looking for a human being, not a lump of meat missing two arms, a leg and half a face with an eye dangling out of its socket. I begged and begged to die—anything for the pain to stop. But yet I had lived through it all. It was a miracle that I had made it past the operation.

I exited the bathroom and strode over to the balcony. The half of my body was that still skin felt the chill of the icy rain as it spat down. The alien buildings of Cyillium stood around me, their glowing lights pulsing vividly as aircrafts sped across the night sky in a straight line. Looking down below I saw myriads of people, scurrying across the wet pavement. Cranking my internal audio enhancers I could every-thing; the shouting of an angry chef as he roasted something in a pot.

The horn of a car, the laughing of friends, the barking of a hungry dog. I heard it all, overpowering my other senses. It was all so...so...*alive*.

I heard the small hum of a camera rotation as Lumen detached herself to a portable device. She floated next to me, almost uncertain of what to say.

"Tell me," I said, "just how am I more human than you?"

"The rain," she said softly as the device's hull got covered in soft droplets. "I know that it's water because it has elements of hydrogen and oxygen. I know it's wet because it's in its liquid state that's neither steam nor snow. I know that it's been condensed from atmospheric water vapor and then precipitated." She paused, as if to take a breath with lungs that didn't exist. "But I'll never know what it really feels like. I'll never know the feeling of moisture on my skin; the cold kiss of water as it cools you down. I'll never experience it for myself." I felt the camera lens shift focus towards me as I stretched out my hand, catching droplets on my fingers. They slid down the thin line on my hand that separated metal from flesh. "You can. But I never will."

Born in 1995 Jeremy Szal *has had over thirty-five publications at* Strange Horizons, Nature's Future, Grimdark Magazine, Fantasy Scroll Magazine *and more. He is also the assistant editor for Hugo winning podcast* StarShipSofa. *He loves coffee, cold weather and lives in Sydney, Australia with his parents, sister, and the world's most hyperactive Jack Russel. Find him at:* https://jeremyszal.wordpress.com/

www.ingramcontent.com/pod-product-compliance
Lightning Source LLC
Chambersburg PA
CBHW071225130626
46555CB00004B/1858